KEEPER

CRYSTALS

Eve and the Fiery Phoenix

For Mum and Dad. Thank you.

First published in the UK in 2017.
This edition published in 2019
by New Frontier Publishing Pty Ltd
Uncommon, 126 New King's Rd, Fulham SW6 4LZ
www.newfrontierpublishing.co.uk

ISBN: 978-0-9956255-2-5 (PB)

Designed by Celeste Hulme

Printed in China
10 9 8 7 6 5 4 3 2

KEEPER OF THE CRYSTALS

Eve and the Fiery Phoenix

Jess Black

Illustrated by Celeste Hulme

'Race you!' Eve took off down the wide footpath that led to the town centre and main beach, her long black curls bouncing madly as she ran. She could hear her friend Oscar sprinting after her. It didn't take him long to catch up.

'Face it, Eve,' Oscar teased, 'you'll never beat *me*!'

Eve scowled as Oscar overtook her. He

1

could be so annoying!

Even though she felt as if her chest might burst, Eve managed to stay on Oscar's tail. They raced each other the four blocks from Eve's grandmother's house to the sleepy main street of Marigold. Oscar reached the low stone wall above the beach ahead of Eve.

'Aaah … you … win!' Eve panted, red-faced, as she drew up beside Oscar. She leaned on the wall to get her breath back.

'Better get used to it,' Oscar quipped.

Eve rolled her eyes and took a swig of water from her drink bottle. Oscar didn't even look puffed, she noticed with irritation.

Oscar and Eve hadn't always liked each other. They had kept their distance until the previous summer, when they had found themselves in danger in the desert of Panthor and Eve had summoned the power of the unicorn. Since then they had become good friends.

'I guess we won't be swimming today,' said Eve, looking out at the bay. It didn't look very welcoming. Dark clouds loomed on the horizon and the wind whipped the frothy white tops of the waves across the sea.

'First rain we've had all holiday,' Oscar said. The sun had shone every day of their Easter break and they had spent most of it in the water. 'Come on,' he said brightly, turning away from the beach. 'Let's go help your gran with the shopping.'

Oscar was very fond of Eve's grandmother Sylvie. The feeling was mutual. He had lived in the house next door to Sylvie all his life.

'Bet I beat you this time!' Eve called and took off, throwing her beach towel over Oscar's head.

Oscar groaned. He pulled the towel off and jogged after her. Being Eve's friend took a *lot* of energy.

The main street in Marigold stretched along the beach and was often busy with people. Eve and Oscar dodged the shoppers and tourists and amused themselves playing tag. Finally they reached the local supermarket. They spotted Sylvie immediately in her bright red frock. She was busy paying at the checkout.

'Anything for us?' asked Oscar with a cheeky grin as he peeked inside Sylvie's shopping bags.

Sylvie smiled. 'Well, I might make some scones when we get home if you play your cards right.'

'Ooh!' Oscar rubbed his stomach in anticipation.

'Go Gran!' Eve put her arm around her

grandmother. There was nothing on Earth like Sylvie's freshly baked scones with jam and cream.

As the electronic doors whooshed open for them to exit, the sky went very dark.

'I don't like the look of those clouds,' Sylvie said, glancing up at the sky.

'I love storms!' Eve exclaimed.

'You won't be saying that when you're completely drenched,' said Oscar drily.

Oscar and Eve carried the groceries as the threesome turned off the main road and headed towards Sylvie's house on Clearview Street. They had only taken a few steps when the sky lit up with a jagged display of lightning and a loud clap of thunder rang out. Rubbish and discarded belongings from the beach began to swirl upwards in the wind.

'Let's get home!' Oscar yelled above the din.

Sylvie shot him a hasty smile and patted Eve on the arm.

'Too far. We'll take shelter.' Sylvie had to raise her voice as the wind grew louder. She pointed down a side street to a narrow brick building standing on its own. Eve couldn't remember ever having seen it before. It looked like a shop and she could see a rusty metal sign swinging wildly in the wind:

'CURIOS. ANTIQUES. ODDITORIUM'.

As they crossed the road the slight spitting of rain turned into a torrential downpour. It was powerful rain that fell in sheets and blew sideways so that it stung Eve's eyes.

They burst into the shop. The door closed behind them with a jingle from a small brass bell. In front of them was a room packed to the rafters with old wares, furniture and interesting objects of all kinds.

'We'll be here for a while,' Sylvie said

with a smile. She sat down in a worn green armchair near the door and began to wring out her hair.

Eve and Oscar looked out through the grimy windows. Eve could hardly see the houses on the other side of the street through the driving rain. Sylvie was right. They would be stuck inside for some time.

'Isn't anybody looking after the shop?' asked Eve. She looked around but couldn't see anyone else in the room.

'It's okay, I know the owner. Wander around,' said Sylvie.

'Cool!' Oscar exclaimed, needing no second invitation to poke around.

Soon the storm was forgotten as Eve and Oscar began to explore. Eve was immediately drawn to a dazzling display of costume jewellery on a table. She still loved playing dress-ups.

'Check this out!' Oscar exclaimed, holding up a small tin robot. Then his eyes lit up as he saw something else and he dashed off.

Eve glanced back at her gran. Sylvie had closed her eyes and looked comfortable. Eve followed Oscar. He had already disappeared into the gloom.

The 'ODDITORIUM' was filled with the most amazing collection of treasures. Most of the stock was in the main entrance but Eve realised that a passage at the back led to many smaller rooms. Oscar had wasted no time in making his way down the shadowy corridor to check them out.

Each room had a different theme. Eve

found one that was like a huge walk-in wardrobe filled with vintage dresses. Never had she seen so many racks of colourful fabrics and sparkling sequins. She was about to try on a dress when she heard Oscar cry out.

Eve hurried down the passage and found him in a room with hundreds of tin soldiers arranged across a huge table. They were set up to act out a battle scene across grass and rolling hills. It looked very lifelike. Oscar was leaning over the table, entranced.

'What's wrong?' Eve asked.

Oscar looked at her with wide eyes. 'It's an enactment of a battle in World War Two. This is incredible! The detail is amazing, and each soldier is unique ... '

'Mmm,' said Eve. Playing soldiers wasn't really her thing. 'Guess you don't want to play dress-ups then?'

10

Oscar didn't answer. He was absorbed in the battle so Eve left him and drifted further down the corridor. At the end a strip of light was shining out from beneath a closed door. Eve walked slowly towards it. She felt unsure about opening the door but then remembered her gran had said they could explore.

With one last look down the corridor Eve turned the shiny brass knob and pushed the door open wide enough to take a peek inside.

The room was filled to the brim with books. The shelves around the walls stretched from the floor right up to the ceiling. Even the window was partly covered with books piled in tall dusty stacks.

'Yikes!' Eve whispered.

Eve loved to read stories and took a moment to walk around the room. The books looked old and most were bound in leather. One book with a scarlet cover and gold writing down the spine caught her eye. Eve pulled the book out. She read the word *Griffid* on the front cover.

Griffid? Eve wondered what it meant.

She opened the book to a random page. It was a sketchbook. On the page was a picture of a bird that was not like any bird Eve had ever seen before. It looked regal. Its long feathers were intricately patterned in rich, vivid colours of scarlet and glittering gold. The beauty of the bird shone through the page.

'Oscar!' Eve called. 'You have to come see this.'

As Eve lifted her hand to turn the page, a sudden flash of lightning illuminated the room. Eve gasped and looked behind her but she was still alone. She felt the hairs on the back of her neck stand on end. 'Get a grip, Eve,' she muttered to herself. It was just the storm.

As she went to replace the book she noticed something tucked at the back of the shelf. She couldn't see what it was but a shard of light caught her eye. Eve felt a rush of energy course through her body. She sucked in her breath. She had felt this way before.

The object was a little glass crystal in the shape of a bird.

Before she knew what she was doing Eve reached out with trembling fingers and touched the smooth surface of the glass bird. The room came alive as light danced around the spines of the books in coloured fractals. The crystal glistened and Eve felt a surge of power like electricity whiz through her body.

13

'What's so exciting that I have to see?' Oscar appeared in the doorway, looking grumpy at being disturbed.

'I … ' Eve stared at the crystal in her hand. She had no memory of picking it up.

Oscar looked at the crystal with shock in his eyes. 'Put it down!' he commanded in a hoarse voice.

'I … I can't!' Eve stammered. She was completely transfixed by the power of the crystal and couldn't move. The crystal had connected to her palm. She knew it would leave a mark. Just like last time.

It was happening all over again. A huge crash of thunder shook the whole shop and the room lit up.

'Eve!' Oscar grabbed her other hand and held it firmly.

Eve braced herself. Last time this had happened she and Oscar had fallen through the air for what felt like hours.

'What's that noise?' Oscar asked, raising his voice. The sound of thunder had morphed into a loud roar. It was deafening and it was coming closer.

'Oscar! Look!'

Eve pointed at the window. They saw a huge wave of water hurtling towards the building. It was utterly terrifying.

'Let's get out of here!' Oscar ran towards the door, pulling Eve with him. As the friends approached the open doorway Eve had a sick feeling that she knew what they would find around the corner.

Hurtling towards them down the corridor was a dark wall of water. Oscar dragged Eve back into the room and slammed the heavy wooden door but within seconds it was torn off its hinges and the dark torrent rushed towards them.

'We're trapped,' Eve yelled.

As the words came out of her mouth the water swept them up and all was blackness.

ve couldn't see anything. The water was dark and moving fast. She had no idea where she was or how deep the water plunged. Her body was tossed around like a sack of straw and she was thrown into somersault after somersault. It felt as though she had been flushed down a giant toilet.

'Help!' she cried out when she surfaced

for breath. But the sound of the water was so loud her words were swallowed up. All around her was pitch black. Where was she? Had there been a tsunami? Eve had no time to wonder as she used all her strength to stay above the rushing water.

'Oscar? Oscar?' Eve listened for a reply but heard nothing. Eve took a gulping breath and tried to quash the panic she felt. Struggling would just tire her out. It was scary but she allowed her body to go limp. She kept her head above the water and sped along with the churning current.

Then, with a bump, Eve collided with a heavy object and clung on to it for dear life. From the feel of it she thought it might be a wooden chair from the shop. She used it to stay afloat.

Time passed in a blur.

Soon Eve's eyes adjusted to the dark and a

landscape began to take shape. Eve realised with a start that the water she was in was completely surrounded by jungle. Thick vines and dense trees crowded the banks on either side of the wide river she was racing down.

Eve saw a shape bumping along in the current, nearer the far bank. She realised it was a tree trunk with something lying across it.

'Oscar!' Eve yelled.

She began to furiously kick her legs. It didn't seem she was making any headway until the river took a sharp turn to the left and she was able to catch up with the log. All of a sudden Oscar was beside her.

'Eve! Grab my arm!' he instructed above the roar of the water.

Eve was terrified to leave her flimsy chair but she stuck out an arm and Oscar grabbed her. She felt herself go under the water again but then she surfaced beside the tree trunk. With one hefty lift Oscar dragged her onto the log and she hugged it tight.

Eve thought she would never feel so happy to see a friend as she did in that moment.

'Thanks,' she managed to say.

'We need to get to the bank. The water's picking up speed!'

Eve realised that they were travelling faster now and the river was becoming narrower. Looking ahead, she saw the jungle end and the river disappear, like an ocean at the end of the world.

'Waterfall!' Eve barked through clenched teeth.

The roar from the water grew more deafening as the two friends kicked with all their might towards the bank. The force of the water was too strong for them. It picked them up like ragdolls and spun them around. Their log was cracking underneath them and the riverbank was growing further away.

'Ah!' Eve cried out in pain as her leg slammed into a rock.

'This is our chance,' shouted Oscar. 'We're going to surf the log.'

'What? Are you crazy?'

But Oscar looked grimly serious. He stood up on the trunk and took a surfing position. Once he had a shaky sense of balance he pulled Eve up beside him. Eve slipped. Her hands gripped the log but she managed to grab Oscar. Together they desperately tried to find their balance. The log rolled jerkily to and fro but did not spin.

'When I say "Now!" you grab hold of me,' Oscar called.

Eve nodded. She was scared to move but

glad that Oscar was taking charge.

'*Now!*'

Just in time Oscar grabbed a low-hanging tree branch and Eve grabbed Oscar. The log shot out from under them. They hung suspended from the branch and it strained under their weight. The water pulled at them and Oscar painfully began to haul them both further and further along the branch towards the riverbank.

'Nearly there,' he gasped.

Eve looked down the river to see the tree trunk shatter into tiny splinters over the rough rocky outcrops, then disappear over the edge of the waterfall.

With one last heave Oscar managed to pull himself up onto the bank. Eve was still in the water clinging to his legs. He snaked his way further up onto the bank, pulling Eve with him, and lay down, exhausted. Eve crawled up onto the grass and lay on her back.

'That was a little close for comfort,' mumbled Oscar.

'You're telling me,' Eve muttered.

They lay on the grassy bank in silence. The river was so loud they couldn't hear anything else except the roar of water. As they got their breath back and Eve's hands stopped shaking they began to take in their surroundings. It was night and through the trees they could see that the moon was nearly full. It cast some light on the thick canopy of vines and trees around them.

'Where are we?'

Eve looked about her and shrugged. 'Some kind of jungle?'

'I'll tell you one thing – we're a world away from home. It's happening all over again, isn't it?' Oscar prompted.

Eve nodded. She opened her palm to reveal the neat imprint of the crystal bird on her hand.

'Oh man,' Oscar sighed and lay back on the ground, closing his eyes.

While Oscar lay still Eve's eyes and ears grew more accustomed to the jungle. She thought she saw movement out of the corner of her eye. A shape materialised from the trees. A huge tiger stalked towards them, slow and powerful.

Eve grabbed Oscar's arm and shook it. He sat up and spotted the tiger.

The creature's tail swished rhythmically from side to side and its green eyes were like deep pools of water. But what Eve couldn't take her eyes off were its paws. They were enormous. One swipe from this cat and she would go flying.

'Maybe it's friendly?' Eve whispered.

The tiger let out a low growl.

Oscar shook his head.

'It's about as far from happy as a tiger can get,' he whispered back.

The tiger growled again. It was a deep guttural sound and it made Eve's blood run cold.

'Tigers can swim and climb trees so there's no point in running away,' said Oscar in a low voice. Eve saw that he was slowly picking up a large stick from the ground beside him.

'What do we do?' asked Eve. She didn't like the look of the tiger – or the stick in Oscar's hand.

'She won't hurt you,' said a boy's voice. 'Unless I tell her to.'

$\mathcal{E}$ ve and Oscar were stunned to see a young boy step out from the thick jungle. He seemed about their age, perhaps a little older, and looked wiry and strong. He wore a simple tunic with a thick leather belt and his feet were bare. His dark shoulder-length hair hung over his eyes.

Oscar stood up abruptly and stepped forward, brandishing his stick.

'Keep away!' he threatened.

'Are you some kind of river demon?' the boy replied calmly, resting his hand on the tiger's head.

'We mean you no harm,' said Eve. She held out her hand. The boy came closer until he could see the outline of the bird on her palm. He inspected it carefully in the dim light. 'Does this mean anything to you?'

It must have meant something to the tiger, who growled again.

The boy's manner changed. He looked at Eve angrily. 'You have the phoenix,' he said sharply. He took a step forward and pulled a carved stick with a pointed end from his belt. He held it out towards them as a weapon.

'Don't come any closer to us,' threatened Oscar and shook his stick at the boy.

'You have taken our sun!' the boy cried.

He looked furious. 'It's thanks to *you* the land is dying.'

'I'm warning you ... ' said Oscar.

The boy kept walking towards them while the tiger drew in closer. They were well and truly trapped.

'Both of you cool it!' said Eve desperately. She stepped between the two boys and held her hands out. 'Let me explain. We aren't demons, we don't have your bird and your sun. We are just like you but somehow I am connected to the bird. If the bird is in trouble I am here to help. This bird, is it in trouble?'

'The phoenix is *gone*!' the boy spat.

'What's a phoenix?' asked Oscar.

The boy pointed to the mark on Eve's hand.

'The bird?' Eve queried.

The boy nodded.

'Please put down your weapon. You can trust us,' Eve told him.

'How can I be sure?'

Eve turned to Oscar, then back to the boy. 'Because the only way for us to get back to our own world will be to find the phoenix,' Eve explained.

'And believe me, living in a dark jungle isn't my idea of a good time,' quipped Oscar.

The boy eyeballed them before giving a gruff nod. He put away his stick. The tiger waited. Its tail swished back and forth impatiently. Oscar lowered his stick.

'Okay.' Eve took a deep breath. 'I'm Eve, and this is Oscar. Can you tell us what is going on?'

'The phoenix is a sacred fire spirit. While the phoenix is free the sun warms our world. It is the most beautiful creature you will ever see.'

'I hope we get to see one,' said Eve, looking around.

'There is only one. It sings a song to the sun every day. Its voice is so beautiful that when it sings it wakes up the sun and the day is born. Without the song of the phoenix the sun cannot rise from its bed.'

'That's impossible!' Oscar burst out. 'That's not how the sun works. The Earth revolves around the sun.'

'Perhaps in your world,' said the boy simply. 'Here it is different.'

'What do you think has happened to the phoenix?' asked Eve.

'Trapped, taken … and ever since then our jungle has been plunged into darkness. Now the plants are dying and people and animals grow sick.'

The tiger growled again. 'He looks pretty healthy to me,' muttered Oscar.

'To make it worse the phoenix is losing feathers. Perhaps to alert us to where it is … but its feathers are flames that start fires. More trees are dying.'

'That's terrible!'

As if on cue a flame shot up into the air like a giant firework. A huge fireball lit up the sky and the jungle around them with a beautiful orange glow before it slowly faded. The three children were once more enveloped in darkness.

'What do we do now?' asked Eve.

'We follow the light,' said the boy.

The boy introduced himself as Slate. 'And this is Tilla.' Slate gave the tiger an affectionate scratch. Tilla rubbed her head against him. There was clearly deep affection between the two.

'She's … beautiful,' said Eve.

Oscar looked completely freaked out, but Eve couldn't help but gawk at Tilla. She had never been so close to such a large and powerful predator. When they had been in Panthor she had spent time with a fully grown panther but Tilla was at least twice as big. Her body was long, her shoulders and back broad, and her strong legs ended in enormous paws that could knock over a human in a second. Her thick coat varied from orange-red to tawny yellow, interspersed with black stripes in different lengths and widths.

Eve held out a hand to Tilla. The tiger stood completely still while Eve touched her thick coat.

Eve turned to Oscar. 'Want to pat her?'

'I'll pass,' he said shakily.

'I will take you to meet my grandfather,' said Slate. 'But stay close. There is danger lurking here in Griffid.'

'Griffid?' Eve remembered the title of the book from the curio shop. 'What is Griffid?'

The boy shrugged. 'Griffid means "tiger jungle". This has been the home of tigers since the beginning. They have lived in harmony with nature. But now there is no balance in the jungle. The tigers kill for pleasure, not just to eat.'

Tilla hissed and struck a clawed paw out at the air.

'Tilla's not happy about this?'

Slate nodded. 'The tiger king rules the jungle. He is Tilla's brother. He banished her. The tigers turned on her because she only kills to eat and says a prayer to the animals and the jungle.'

Eve shivered. She realised her clothes were still wet and the night air had a distinct chill.

'We should begin walking,' said Slate. 'You look cold.'

They set off with Tilla in the lead. Eve

followed, with Slate and Oscar behind her. It was slow going. The jungle floor was a mass of roots and vines, and the brush was so thick and tangled that they had to navigate around it.

Even so, Eve found herself relaxing in Slate's company as they walked together. The same couldn't be said for Oscar. He didn't stop scowling from the moment they set off. Eve shot him a meaningful look which he characteristically ignored.

Eve was interested to hear more about Slate. 'Have you always lived here?' she asked.

Slate nodded. 'A small tribe of humans live in the forest. We are permitted to by the tigers as we are, *were*, guardians of the phoenix. I feel even more to blame for what has happened because it was our duty to protect the sacred bird.'

'Mistakes happen,' smiled Oscar.

Slate ignored the interruption.

'We don't know who took the phoenix but it happened at night. It was dark, there was no moon and I had fallen asleep at my post.'

Oscar clapped Slate on the back and gave him a look of commiseration.

'We think it must have been the tiger king but he lives a long way away and he's very dangerous.'

'So where are we going?' Oscar asked.

'First we are going to my home. It's where the guardians of the phoenix live.'

***

They walked for a long time. Eve grew increasingly tired and hungry, and felt cold right down to her bones. She began to fall

36

behind the others.

Oscar noticed. He slowed down and held Eve's arm to help her walk. 'How far now?' he asked Slate.

'Not long,' the boy replied.

Oscar was silent for a moment, then he stopped walking. 'But how do we know we can trust *you*?' he asked with an edge to his voice.

Slate stopped. The boys locked eyes.

'Turn around slowly to your left,' whispered Slate. 'No sudden moves.'

'What now?' Oscar was growing tired of Slate and his commands. 'You're not the boss, you know.'

Tilla let out a low and throaty growl.

Eve sucked in her breath. 'Do what he says, Oscar.'

Oscar turned his head slowly to see a brightly coloured snake coiled around a

37

branch just near his head. It was red with black and white bands. Oscar knew enough about snakes to know this one looked highly poisonous. The snake looked at him with beady eyes and stretched its neck out closer to him.

'Don't move,' warned Slate.

'Easy for you to say,' murmured Oscar.

'Just listen very carefully to my voice,' continued Slate. 'These snakes strike if frightened. We don't want to alarm it. Everything is okay.'

Eve's heart raced. Yet there was nothing she could do to help but stay as still as she could.

The snake hissed. Its shaking tongue came closer to Oscar's face. Oscar's eyes darted this way and that but he kept still.

'Trust me,' Slate murmured. 'When I call out I want you to drop to the ground.'

38

All of a sudden there was a rush of air next to Oscar's ear.

'Now!' Slate yelled.

Oscar ducked just as Tilla pounced on the snake, containing it with her heavy claws.

'Leave here,' Slate commanded.

Tilla retracted her claws and lifted her paw, releasing the snake. The snake crawled away into the depths of the greenery.

Oscar let out a deep sigh of relief.

'Thank you,' he managed to say, and he meant it. 'I think we can trust you now.'

s soon as Eve saw an inviting light shining through the dappled leaves she felt a little better.

'Welcome to my home,' said Slate.

He gave a low whistle and a few seconds later it was answered by two similar calls.

Slate pulled back the foliage with Oscar's help and they stepped through the low entrance to a cave. Inside it was rough but homey. An older man was seated cross-legged on the floor. He looked like Slate but had grey hair and a beard.

'This is my grandfather, Elek.'

Slate introduced Eve and Oscar. Elek looked at them closely, then clasped his hands as if he was praying and gave a bow.

'You look just like your grandmother,' he said to Eve.

Eve's jaw dropped. 'How do you know my gran?'

'Ah,' Elek nodded with a smile, 'a long time ago, when I was a young boy, it was Sylvie who came.'

Eve shook her head in confusion. It was hard to imagine her gran being anything but the old lady she knew her to be. Sylvie had been an *adventurer*?

She met Oscar's glance but he looked equally stunned. Eve suddenly felt wide awake, her brain zinging with unanswered questions.

'Why did Gran come here?' asked Eve. 'Was she alone?'

'I think that's a story that *she* will need to tell you.' Elek clapped his hands together. 'May I see your hand?'

He reached out a hand and Eve held hers out for him to see. 'It's as I thought,' he said slowly as his finger traced the shape of the phoenix on Eve's hand. 'I think the phoenix has summoned you. We are the bird's guardians but we have failed. Without the phoenix the sun sleeps and without the sun we will all perish.'

Eve gulped.

'What do you mean?' asked Oscar.

Elek continued. 'We have been without the sun for only two days but it is getting colder by the day. After one week it will

42

snow, and then … '

Elek didn't finish the sentence.

Eve shivered. Elek rubbed her hand.

'Come. You are cold, my child.' Elek gave Slate some instructions for finding a change of clothes for Eve and Oscar. 'We'll get you warm and then eat some food.'

'I don't see how we can help,' said Eve as she took a seat on the floor.

Elek expertly set about lighting a fire. 'If we find the tiger king then we find the phoenix. That's if it's still alive. And your arrival gives us an advantage. You have powerful magic, Eve. I've seen it before.'

Tilla let out a yowl that made the hairs on the back of Eve's neck stand up.

'Tilla knows where to find the tiger king,' said Slate coldly, 'whether the king likes it or not.'

'Tigers love the night,' Elek explained.

'The sun reveals the hunters to their prey. The tiger king resents the phoenix for waking the sun.'

'Great!' observed Oscar. 'So we just have to beat a dangerous rogue tiger, rescue the phoenix and get the sun to shine or we'll all freeze to death.'

Elek nodded seriously. 'That's it in a nutshell.'

***

Elek ordered Slate, Eve and Oscar to rest. Despite the urgent need to find the phoenix, Eve knew she needed sleep.

They slept for five hours and when Elek woke them they set off again into the darkness. It was with a heavy heart that Eve left the small and cosy cave for the dark and foreboding jungle. The crystal had connected her to the phoenix, but would she be strong enough to defeat the tiger king?

As they picked their way through the dense vegetation, Eve's thoughts turned to the people of Griffid. She wondered what life would be like without the sun. She had never liked rainy weather that forced her to stay indoors but that was nothing compared to permanent darkness. She'd never really thought about how much life depended on the sun and how much she took it for granted.

Their progress was slow through the jungle. The ground was covered in decaying leaves and all the bugs, spiders, scorpions, snakes and slithering things that can make life miserable for a human. Elek had to look carefully for vines and Slate helped Eve and Oscar climb over the low-lying masses.

It was weird being in the dark for so long. Eve kept expecting the sun to rise. Everything looked a little creepier. Scarier. Despite her change of clothes Eve felt cold. It wasn't just her imagination – it *was* getting colder. She hoped they found the tiger king soon.

And the phoenix.

They were running out of time.

Suddenly Eve felt a surge of heat rip through her body. It took her breath away. Her hand felt hot and the mark throbbed. Eve knew that the phoenix was alive.

'The phoenix!' she gasped. 'It's here.'

*E*lek and Slate stopped in their tracks. Tilla hissed. Her enormous sharp teeth flashed white in the dark. She looked ready for a fight.

'Do you think the sacred bird is still alive?' Elek asked.

Eve nodded. 'The signal is weak but it's there.'

'It all adds up. We're close to the ambush,'

Slate said to his father.

'Do you know something we don't?' asked Oscar with suspicion.

'An ambush is the name given to a group of tigers,' Slate explained. 'This has always been their hunting ground. There is a labyrinth of caves here called the caves of Merden.'

'But you are right, Oscar,' Elek added. 'We don't want to walk into an ambush. We're facing a large group of dangerous tigers. We need the element of surprise.'

'Wait,' said Eve. She closed her eyes and silently tried to communicate with the phoenix. She had to concentrate very hard. *Where are you?* she asked the bird, without speaking.

A second later Eve's eyes snapped open as a fireball shot into the air. A dance of colours lit up the sky then exploded in a cascade of a thousand sparkles.

'You wanted to know if the phoenix is still alive?' smiled Oscar. 'There's your sign.'

'That fire came straight out of the caves of Merden,' Elek said hurriedly. 'The caves are a maze. They are the perfect place for the tiger king to keep the phoenix. The sun will never hear it down there. We need to get to it – and soon.' He sprang into action. 'Eve, Oscar, Slate: we four will stick together while Tilla acts as a decoy. Tilla, we need you to lure the tigers away.'

Tilla growled in agreement.

Elek gave Tilla a friendly pat. 'Stay downwind and let them pick up your scent. They will come to you. Remember you are a decoy, Tilla. You don't want a fight. Just keep them running.'

The tiger gave another low growl.

'Good luck,' said Oscar. He reached out

and gently stroked the beast.

Slate locked eyes with Tilla and nodded to her. It was time.

Tilla vanished silently into the darkness.

Elek put his finger to his lips and began to walk in the direction of the caves.

Eve's palm burned. The mark of the phoenix glowed and she felt a burst of lightness and energy. Her whole body felt warm as if she was sitting in front of a toasty fire. It was a good sign.

They moved as one as they crept closer and closer to the caves. Eve noticed they were heading up a slope and she could see a mountain in the distance. Once the caves were in view they crouched down so they could not be seen over the low foliage. Four tigers lounged sleepily on the ground. Two others were finishing off a kill.

'They are mean-looking tigers,' Oscar

50

whispered.

'Much bigger than Tilla,' Eve said.

'She is fast and clever. She is a leader, not a follower,' whispered Slate in defence of his tiger friend.

They waited nervously until Tilla came into view. The tiger's stripes blended seamlessly into the background. She waited patiently a short distance from the caves.

The other tigers smelled her before they saw her. The six large tigers at the front of the caves bounded off into the bushes in hot pursuit. They were followed by three smaller tigers who appeared out of the trees.

'That's not the whole ambush. There must still be more inside protecting the tiger king,' Elek noted.

Eve felt her heart racing in her chest. She touched the mark on her hand to calm herself and her palm burned intensely. The swell of energy surged through her again. She spoke to the phoenix once more in her mind.

We are here to rescue you, do you understand? Eve told the phoenix. A faint image of the bird came into her head. It was more beautiful than she could have imagined. But it looked really ill, not at all how it had appeared in the sketchbook. Its head drooped and its eyes were listless. For the first time the bird spoke to Eve.

Hurry. I need you.

Eve heard the words but they weren't spoken. They were sung in a voice as melodic and rich as any she had ever heard. It was like listening to bells chiming, or her mother singing her a lullaby.

Eve sensed how urgently they needed to get to the bird. She took the lead and crept to the opening of the cave. She saw a dim glow of light coming from deeper inside. A quick look in the cave revealed there was no tiger near the entrance.

'Come on,' she whispered to the others, beckoning them to follow.

Once inside, they found two distinct paths leading off from the central room. Each narrow passage wormed its way into the depths of the mountain.

'We have to split up,' whispered Eve. 'The signal from the phoenix is so weak I can't tell which way to go.'

Oscar shook his head. 'It's too dangerous.'

'We don't have time. We have to hurry.' Eve hastily made her way down the passage to the left.

'You go with her,' Elek signalled to Oscar. 'Slate and I will take the other path.'

'Eve, wait!' Oscar hissed and hurried to catch up with her. They had no idea what

53

was waiting from them in the darkness ahead.

*E*ve walked fast. She tried to put her fear of the tiger king to the back of her mind. She focused her thoughts on the phoenix.

Hurry. Follow the music.

Eve paused. She couldn't hear anything except the sound of her and Oscar's breathing. It was stuffy and airless in the caves and getting hotter by the second. But as they wound their way deeper into the hill Eve thought she could hear music. It was faint but unmistakeable. The phoenix was calling to her.

'Can you hear that?' she asked Oscar.

Oscar shook his head.

Was the song playing for Eve's ears only? It meant the bird trusted her to save it. Eve broke into a run and then a sprint. She darted this way and that, with Oscar following close behind.

Be careful.

A sudden opening in the passage hit Eve with a blast of hot air and a ringing of melody. The phoenix. Oscar and Eve just stood and stared.

The phoenix was the most beautiful creature Eve had ever seen. It looked a bit like an eagle in size and appearance but the way it held its head reminded her of an elegant swan. At first it appeared to be made of gold but as Eve's eyes adjusted she realised it was multicoloured – gold and purple and yellow. It had huge majestic wings on either side of its body and a long plume of feathers behind it that took up most of the cave. But the bird had lost many of its feathers. They lay strewn on the floor around it.

'It's incredible,' Oscar gasped.

Now that she was looking at it Eve remembered where she had seen the bird before. It was a mythical creature they had learned about at school. It was known as a firebird.

'Come with me.' Eve showed the bird her palm.

The phoenix turned its regal head, opened its beak and sang. The tune was mesmerising. Eve felt utterly entranced. Yet the song was so sad that tears formed in her eyes. The bird was dying.

'Let's get you back outside,' coaxed Eve. She motioned to Oscar to help her lift the bird.

As they approached it a roar filled with hate and bile cut through the air and silenced the bird's song.

The tiger king. He was flanked by two smaller tigers.

The tiger king was enormous. He stepped from a hidden opening in the side of the cave and padded menacingly towards Eve, looming over her small frame. He was hungry for a fight.

Eve straightened. Her mouth felt dry and it was difficult to speak. Her voice came out in a whisper. 'We're taking the phoenix.'

Eve held out her palm towards the tiger.

The mark on her hand burned a brilliant red.

The king shook his enormous head and let out another roar. He lunged at Eve, claws extended. His paw just missed her nose. Eve stumbled back and found herself pressed up against the opposite wall beside the phoenix.

'Don't you get it? You'll all die without the sun!' Oscar stepped in front of Eve. He looked around for something to use as a weapon but the room was bare except for the feathers.

The tiger came closer still. Oscar held his breath but stood his ground.

Eve realised the bird couldn't help. It was too weak. They were on their own. She looked around desperately. If only there was something else that could help them! But there was only …

Feathers!

Slate had mentioned the bird's feathers catching fire. Perhaps that was how it had signalled to them! She looked up and saw a small hole in the roof. The bird must have been throwing feathers into the sky …

The tiger king let out a deafening roar. Eve couldn't help but notice how huge his jaw and sharp teeth were. She braced herself.

'I have the mark of the phoenix. You thought you could contain it but you have only made it more powerful.'

There was a rush of footsteps and Elek and Slate appeared in the doorway. 'Eve!' Slate yelled and pulled out his crude sword.

The tiger was distracted for a second and Eve saw her chance. She threw herself to the ground and grabbed a handful of feathers.

'Here!' Eve flung a few at Oscar. 'Do what I do.'

The tiger king roared in anger and got ready to pounce. The small space echoed with the roar of tigers. It gave Eve the moment she needed.

'Now!' Eve yelled. She threw the feathers, as hard as she could, like darts at the tigers. Oscar did the same. They flew through the air and burst into flame. The fireballs sizzled on the tiger king's coat and pierced his skin. He howled and fell, roaring in anger. Elek and Slate gathered up more feathers and held them at the ready. One tiger let out a howl of pain and took off. The other dropped its head meekly. Only the tiger king remained defiant until Slate and Elek had him surrounded.

'We have to get the phoenix outside – quickly!' Eve cried. The bird had lost consciousness and lay still.

Oscar and Eve managed to pick up the

bird and carry it back along the passage. Elek and Slate moved behind the tiger king, holding out the phoenix feathers, and prodded him along behind Eve.

Once outside, Eve and Oscar lay the phoenix on a soft bed of leaves. It lay very still, its breathing short and raspy.

Eve stroked the beautiful feathers with her hand. She felt the energy of the crystal pass through her palm to the bird. Then suddenly the phoenix raised its wings and took off. It flew immediately to the highest tree and landed on an exposed branch. It bathed the area below it in a soft light.

'You can do it. Sing for the sun,' Eve whispered.

Just as the words were out of her mouth the phoenix and the branch it was perched on burst into flames.

$\mathcal{A}$s they all watched the fire in disbelief, Tilla arrived. She looked utterly exhausted but she was most definitely alive.

'Looks like you've lost your tigers,' Slate said, giving Tilla a rub on the head.

The large cat's eyes flashed. She had played her role perfectly.

The fire enveloped the whole tree and

climbed higher and higher. A huge ball of flame shot out into the air like fireworks and lit up the jungle around them.

'Keep watching,' Eve said. Her face was filled with a sudden hope. She had just remembered what else they had learned at school about the phoenix.

Eventually the flames died down. Only hunks of burned wood and a few embers remained. There was no more phoenix and the night was still black and endless.

'We're done for,' Elek said.

'No, look!' Oscar pointed.

What had looked like a lump of charcoal shook off a layer of ash, revealing beautiful crimson feathers. It raised its voice to the sun.

The phoenix had been reborn. It began to sing and its voice was even more heavenly than before.

'The phoenix is reborn every five hundred years. It burns but rises again from the ashes,' Eve said.

As Eve spoke the sun came out. At first it was nothing more than a subtle pink glow, but soon dappled colour and light spread across the vegetation.

Elek addressed the tiger king. 'Your night hunting days are over. No more will you terrorise this jungle and kill for fun. You will stay and protect the phoenix and you will serve your new leader. Queen Tilla.'

The tiger king looked like a king no more. His coat was scorched and in the light of day he looked older and much less powerful.

The sun felt warm on Eve's skin. She was happy to bask in its beauty and listen to the sound of a bird singing its morning song to the sun.

Griffid was a very different place when the sun shone. Eve and Oscar stayed in Slate and Elek's cave home and enjoyed getting to know their new friends and their life in the jungle.

Oscar and Slate went fishing together most days in Slate's wooden kayak.

Eve roamed the jungle with Tilla.

Elek stayed behind and watched over the old tiger king and the phoenix.

Each morning they were woken just before daybreak by the tinkling sound of the phoenix singing to the sun. It was the most unearthly and harmonious sound – a choir of angels, bells, wind chimes and mystical tones.

The sun rose over the treetops and the land was bathed in a golden glow. It never grew old.

And then it was time to go home.

Eve gave Elek and Slate a warm goodbye hug.

'We'll never forget you,' she promised. 'Every time I see the sun I'll think of Griffid.'

'We'll miss you.' Slate said solemnly.

'Give my best to your gran,' Elek said with a twinkle in his eye. Eve laughed.

Tilla gave the pair an affectionate nudge which was so powerful it knocked Oscar to the ground.

Eve stroked the downy feathers of the phoenix. The firebird trilled with pleasure. There was no need for words. Eve heard the song the bird sang for her. She knew she would never forget the tune. She took Oscar's hand and looked at the mark on her palm. Home.

***

The old curio shop was the same as when they had left it. It bore no sign that it had been swamped by a wave of water. Eve and Oscar found themselves back in the room where Eve had touched the crystal. The sketchbook was still there but the crystal was nowhere to be seen.

'My gran has some explaining to do,' Eve announced to Oscar.

He raised an eyebrow but said nothing. When Eve had made a decision about something she was not easily swayed.

As they entered the main shop Eve could hear gentle snoring. Sylvie was fast asleep in the green chair near the door.

'Gran!'

Sylvie looked up, startled.

'Oh, I must have dozed off,' she said drowsily.

'While you've been asleep we've surfed a

raging river, fought a vicious tiger king and saved the golden phoenix.' Eve studied her gran's face intently.

'Sounds like you had a few dreams of your own!' exclaimed Sylvie.

'Uh-uh! You don't get off so easily,' Eve continued. 'Does the name Elek mean anything to you?'

Sylvie's face grew serious. She leaned back slowly in her chair. 'I did know an Elek once, a long time ago.'

'I know,' Eve announced triumphantly. 'He told me I look like you!'

Sylvie nodded her head thoughtfully. 'The Elek I knew lives a long way away, almost in another world.' She gave a wistful smile.

Eve nodded. 'Yes! In Griffid. We were *there*.' She pointed to Oscar. 'And we almost died!'

'You look alright to me,' Sylvie said,

looking Eve up and down and winking at her.

'What about the book back there? How come you sheltered from the storm in *this* shop?' Eve demanded.

Sylvie shrugged but said no more as she gathered her things together. She looked out the window.

'Looks as if the storm has passed. We should be getting home now.' She opened the door and the bell gave a little tinkle as it closed behind her.

'Aaah!' Eve stomped her foot on the floor of the shop. 'She's impossible.'

'Like someone else I know,' said Oscar with a smile.

Eve scowled at him.

'Maybe she has a good reason for not talking about the crystals and the magic,' Oscar considered. 'Maybe it's to protect us.'

'Maybe ... '

'Come on, let's go home,' said Oscar, holding the door open for Eve as she picked up the bags of groceries. 'Maybe your gran will still make scones. I'm starving!'

Eve watched her grandmother walk slowly down the footpath ahead of them. What secrets did she carry with her that she couldn't share? Eve burned to know the truth.

She was determined to get the full story out of her gran. She just had to figure out how.

ABOUT THE AUTHOR

Jess Black enjoys writing stories with heaps of action and humour. She has previously co-written *The Bindi Wildlife Adventure Series*, a fictional series about helping endangered animals around the world.

Now available in the series

For more riddles and
adventures visit
www.keeperofthecrystals.com.au